Chronicles of the King

The Coming of the Bear

An Epic War Poem

By

Michael de Angelo

Gododdin Publishing
San Francisco ~ London

First Printing 2009

For the life of one child...

chronicles of the king

the coming
of
the bear

Then was a splintering of shields, the sea wolves coming on in war-whetted anger. Again, the spears burst breast-lock, breached life-wall of Weird-singled men. Wistan went forth that Wurstan fathered, fought with the warriors where they thronged thickest. Three he slew before the breath was out of Offa's body.

It was a stark encounter, but they held their ground – the warriors in that fight fought till wounds dragged them down. The dead fell. All the while Eadwold and Oswald his brother cried on their kinsmen, encouraging them to stand up under the stress, strike out the hour, weaving unwavering the web of steel.

Then Brythwold spoke, shook ash spear, raised shieldboard. In the bravest words this hoar-companion handed them the charge:

Courage shall grow keener, clearer the will, the heart fiercer, as our force faileth.

- Anon

...Britain...A.D. 488, the dying days of the Roman Empire. The Roman Catholic Church, using hundreds of its scribes, has appropriated and forever altered for its own ends the teachings of first century Christianity...only three copies of the original gospels are to escape the Roman purge, to be sought throughout history.

Civilization looks over the precipice into the yawning chasm of the approaching Dark Ages. On the continent of Europe, in Russia and Asia, marauding barbarians are destroying civilization, burning every church and library. The classical learning of the ages must take refuge in the few stone towers of the Irish monks who would protect it, awaiting its emergence almost a thousand years later as the flowering of the Renaissance. The true gospels will vanish for a yet longer time.

Between this last solitary flame of civilization and the barbarians who seek to extinguish it stands one man, perhaps, one battle. He seeks the impossible, to bring his cavalry over a mountain ridge by night, to surprise at dawn four thousand Saxon infantry on the plain below...

To history, he would come to be known as King Arthur. In his own time, this giant was known as Arturus, the Bear.

i am firstborn,
warrior of a new nation,
torchbearer
of an invisible tribe
in unceasing revolution
for restoration
of sacred dominion

i am hammer
and forge the sweord
that is the blood
that births the nation
that carries us,
that carries us on

Distant Fires

21 November, A.D. 488

        this wind   flies   from nowhere
     not a raven   dares risk wing   descends
    no element's kindred   no scion of these hills
   the four quarters could not claim it   or any
age fall upon its dwelling place. Come the night, it
hunts its breed, but it will find no kinsmen here. Were
there no greater hour to meet it, I still could not go
forth – I am not yet its equal.

Lone flame, glow in the branch pile, hands
bitten cold. The *fyr* young, hissing to open palms,
flames yet too small...better warmed by breath.

Red sweords break the dawns – the heavens
must soon protest. Fortnight by fortnight the swollen
river rages redder, blights the land that bore it. No
crop escapes *fyr*, no village, sweord.

Who is conquered? Who, victorious? Killing,
we find our death. Attacking their homeland, ours is
laid waste. Fallen children, how many? Women dead,
who yet counts the number? Who praises now the
greatness of armies?

Our endless coasts we cannot defend. Why will
they not meet us on the field? Why will they not come
forth? Evade us, then. I wait no longer. I make war
now on the offensive for you who are soon the feel the
season of my reaping!

Shadow of frost on the wood melts. Sitting by
red flames on frozen earthrock, fingers rubbed by
fingers, high above the land in the straining
winds...this is no earthly cold. Once, I joined the war.
Now I am the war. Ride a hundred tribes across the
  island, chieftains armed to do my bidding, yet we

do not advance, and victory is denied us. A half-score settlements stormed, skirmishes, brief battles, but their clans still roam at larger, rarely seen, never joined on the battleplain.

Overhead, vast expanse no comfort, but the awesome warning of infinity. Blood heavens now, the blackness itself burns red before battle. Stronger stars intone one chant above the clamorous quiet of the multitude. I am a free man, but I do not choose.

Thick smokesmell of pine, crackling yellow and blue flame tongues leaping now, hands warming... chains of black clouds passing before the red moon.

Where have the years gone? Memories arising seem not my own. Only moment by moment I endure. All that once was, can never return, more distant than a midnight dream. Why do I seek it out? What I once possessed, what once possessed me, could it have been so true? That *woruld* I first beheld, glowing in the nearness of a knowable God...

Waiting in a barren hollow of this ridge, high above two night-shrouded valleys behind and before me, *fyr's* light consumes the darkness around, until only its light is seen. Distant things surrounding once moonlight and shadow grow invisible. The flames are story-filled, gateways I want –

Death is the lord now – that is why we live. I know the path that has brought us here. What path grants us safe return? I have led us too far on this narrow way among the cliffs, even as the sea rises behind us, and our cries drown in crashing waves' fierce foundry.

In truth, our lord has left us, fled from false fighting. Fear joins us now a constant companion.

The flames climb *strang* now, burning unbroken by gusts...a gale that gains succor with God, or the enemy. The flames cannot feel it – only it blows across our backs...

It was another who lived those wars, long ago, so very young to know only the glory of arms...so very wise, I thought. Only, battles won were never truly won, returning now wreckage storm-wrought on the seas, shattered rock-strewn, advancing on the tides.

All I have destroyed appears again to my eyes... thousands of faces dread-carved, driven under horses' hooves bone trampling, first fallen in fear of my coming, their flight hopeless! Fools who falsely claim arms still-stricken by swift sweord stroke! I had no need to kill, only take their lives – but I drank of Saxon blood and was nourished. Early graves for the weak! Who will take this land from the tribes?

Only smoldering...do you hunger? Here, wood for you, and more to come...

I will give quarter to the man who speaks to me of justice but let him dishonor a hearth-companion and he will find no end to my wrath on earth.

Dry wrathful storm, would you blow us from *fyr* and ridge? I pray the digging goes well below...

Who knows what claim a warrior has to this land? This land alive that breathes with all the generations of forgotten men and women who have labored to make us, their children, their weariness and their pain...centuries of hearts through the cold and

3

rain, our mother and fathers, land that sees, unspeaking now.

This ground...hallowed by the burial mounds and barrows of our ancestors. Will they remember us, hear us now in our time of peril? How loud need be our cries? Do you await our summoning, dead of countless years, who have loved this land far longer than we? Come, let your clans throng again upon the moors.

Our own sons will not praise us, could never know the toll of lives, the hardships that we have borne that they might find some peace in this, their decades of passage. Our children will forget us, deny us as barbarians, more, killers – for truth, we are *strang*, living by the beast, in our warring and our worship, but we do not make of ourselves what we are not. Grace alone grants the animal, God.

Cold dwells in my chest. The *fyr* can drive it only from my hands and feet. I cherish warmth, but I would not live by it. There is a coming darkness, who can deny it?

The great war will come. We can only ready ourselves. Already fathers cast out sons, sons hate, and mothers fear their daughters. Clan falls upon clan, forgetful of any greater hope – the church is unworthy of worship. They gave us this, our fathers who so loved the Romans.

Blood ties have fallen, while no stronger loyalty has come to serve in their stead. They did their *weorc* well, when the hearts of once *strang* tribesmen hold no greater allegiance than to the great civilization, the

4

Roman way, but I am yet lord to ten thousand men whom the Weirds would cast adrift without me.

Far below on the plains, *fyrs* of the enemy camp, a thousand lighted caverns in the surrounding gray.

Glow the savage *fyrs* without number, but I will build the clans anew, clans within clans, within tribes, within nation, and the nation will know no government but devotion to the peace and the fury of the unborn race, the coming generations whose hearts and minds will be so unlike ours, not driven and divided, who will join voice with the wolves and not fear them.

So will the burden of the darkness within be released, no longer carried a living death.

So will they surpass us who would be civilized while bringing violence to all we see and think and speak, our will to kill, the birth of our every desire.

War is in the blood of us all. The tribes could not stand united a fortnight without the common enemy.

How long before they rise in arms against one another? Cold, hunger, and strange sweords keep the clans. These are my troops and my charge. So grow the savage rumblings beneath this island. This land lies as a serpent upon the seas, and all tribes and nations will one day bear its strike.

Our blood, stirring to ancient memories rooted in the soil, while the history of the nation comes to us another legacy. Great gray-walled cities, terraces and canals across the countryside, roads of paving stones through deep forests, the lighthouses upon the dark windswept bays – she protected us, she let us prosper.

She gave us order, her arms, her wealth and her government...the Roman island.

I think the sacrifice too great. Mighty city, where now your dreams of *woruld* conquest? Where now the great civilization? You learned too late the power of the mounted warrior.

The Goths rode the returning ghosts of your own cruelties, and even the imperial walls could not stand against them. No, it is not that I do not see your glory...only, I could never forget all you destroyed in claiming your victory.

Mighty Rome, you came, assembling the greatest fighting force ever known. Conquering the tribes of the east, to gather at the foot of the mountains that led into the western regions – where the tribes of the Silurians and Ordovicans gathered, along with all those who knew peace with Rome another name for servitude. Mighty Rome, you conquered.

Those early years that were to begin three centuries of occupation...worthy Caradog, warring for nine years in the western mountains, then captured and dragged like a beast through the streets of Rome. Even then, when all was lost, you were greater than misfortune, walking with neither fear nor sorrow, nor condescension; you behaved with dignity amidst ruin and conquest.

Even to the emperor you spoke your proud defiance. What Briton could ever forget your words? 'Ambitious Rome aspires to universal dominion. Must all mankind, therefore, bend their necks to the yoke? I stood at bay for years. Had I acted otherwise, where would have been your glory of conquest? Where would have been my honor of brave resistance?'

...Bodica, Queen of the Iceni, our kings will forever bear with you their insult, forever remember your vengeance...a loyal Roman Briton, your husband, to leave his inheritance to the empire. The troops that came to collect the tribute flogged you, sacked your palace, and raped your daughters.

How foolish of them to think your tribesmen loyal Romans, too, to think lightly of a woman's rage – you gathered your followers to slaughter the soldiers settled on your land, routing the ninth legion...into your hands and your wrath fell Londinium, then Verualamium. No prisoners taken, but three score thousand put to sweord and crucified, two cities razed by *fyr* to their ramparts, yet forever bearing your dark signature. It took the might of the continental army to quell your uprising – even your suicide, triumphant, and your followers fighting on.

Great Rome, where did you march? To Anglesey, to Anglesey. Land of the Druids, our priests, our teachers and our seers, the memory, the voice and vision of our tribes. So did you break the resistance on the western frontier...great courage to cut their throats, and burn the sacred oak graves. So the tribes were made weak, and darkness overcame them.

Ground beneath me, cold, hard. How fares this night's task?

Names I learned as a child coming alive to haunt me...Carausius, of the sea-faring tribes of the North Sea, mercenary commander of the Roman fleet, clearing the trade routes of pirates, only to take his ships to this island and declare himself emperor of the whole Roman empire. With the control of the seas, this island was made an impenetrable fortress.

Were it that our enemies were across the seas now...his sailors those many generations past settled the Saxon shore. Now more are born, and more of that hated tribe land here yearly.

He showed the nation its power, and planted the seeds of its upheaval.

Constantius, marching to Rome with the garrison of our island...his conquest was great, but his legacy so weakened us, spawning hosts of kings who would dream the imperial dream, hosts of kings and generals who would be emperors, sacrificing the fate of their own nation to know a few seasons of lordship over Rome's dying dominions.

Even Maximus, calling our finest soldiers to continental glory, later to summon the few that remained, while Hadrian's wall after these hundred years still lies unoccupied, forts and signal stations undefended. The poets wrought lays of the conquering general, but for the warrior tribesmen who remained to withstand the onslaught of the barbarian invasions, the memories were of deserted barracks, empty camps and grass-covered roads.

There were few who had remained to fight, and the slaughter upon the homeland was great...that time not unlike our own...kingdoms free of external rule, casting off what remained of the institutions and laws of Rome to make local wars, tyrants arising, still wearing the ensigns of her royalty, but without decency or lawful right, seditious generals and wayward soldiery plotting the success of their own ambitions. But soon there was no time for lesser wars.

Before a generation had passed, the enemies of Britain formed the Barbarian Alliance, powerful, relentless, victorious. The kings of the island were forced to grant them peace and land...although it was only land they wanted.

The raids continued and strikes from the sea for a hundred years. The Saxons alone could never have given us such worthy battle, those barbarian tribes who first came as allies of Rome, to fight her wars, to protect her provinces. When the Franks and the Attacotti joined the alliance, not even the united kingdoms could stand against them. Barbarians everywhere looted the towns, roaming roads at will, slaying and making slaves of the fleeing refugees who filled the streets.

By the *fyr*, my companions not as restless as I.

Now, nearly forsaken by the present, it seems the past alone can lead us to the safe pathways of the future...

Rome came, again...the last time the prows of her rescuing warships would ever be seen on the eastern horizon, the last time the sounds of her bugles would be heard on the morning silence.

Her soldiers came upon horses, feet stirrup-bound. The newly formed cavalry was no longer only a skirmishing guard, a scavenger for the infantry. She had learned from her conquerors, how to fight on

9

horseback, secured by stirrup, clad in the new ring armor, awakening the barbarians from their too early dream of conquest, turning the war back into their own homelands.

The tribesmen found hope, believing order would be restored, believing Rome, the great imperial city, might rule once again...but as swiftly as she had come, she left. Theodosius took his troops back to the continent.

This century opened with growing peril, the military weak, the cities decaying. With unreliable treaty troops and the hungry mercenaries of a dying empire patrolling the provinces, the shield of Hadrian's wall was broken forever, leaving only the continuing onslaughts of the barbarians visible on the horizon...

Why were our kings so blind, the nation so deaf to the voices of the time? Every omen had warned them to seek a new destiny away from the disintegrating continent, where armies fought like wolves for the remains of the fallen empire. With Rome the great city sacked, the prize of eight centuries of ambition and glory overrun, the heathen hordes wandered and rode fearlessly the extent of her dominions. Still, she sought imperial glory, unmindful of her own defense.

Again, another Briton arose to proclaim himself emperor, departing for the continents with the nation's troops.

The tribesmen rebelled, deposing his deputies, taking control of the government, organizing the first army of the nation.

They were separate and scattered tribes no longer, the land for the first time seeing itself in unity, one in army and council, capable of holding a unified policy long after the Roman administration that once bound them together had crumbled. Britons holding office by British law. Britain, the nation. Rome would never return, and we looked to our own defense.

The *weorc* songs grow nearer...my captains driving on the road builders.

How many times had the Roman cavalry shown swift and bloody vengeance to our invaders, only to have them return as soon as their troops were withdrawn?

It was our own troops that needed to form, freeing us of our helplessness and our dependence, granting us some hope of withstanding the barbarian onslaught.

From Rome, we learned cavalry warfare, the forging of armor, the beginning of discipline...and a taste of power...

Could I only remember all that was told to me as a child...

Many of the Saxons were still raiders, then, until Vortigernus brought them here to settle as treaty troops, mercenary warriors...how could he have been so foolish, his means so desperate, his resources so depleted? Even seeking help from Rome, when that giant was already on its knees. Was he hoping for a revival of Roman rule? The troops of Theodosius had been gone nearly a hundred years. Was his faith so great in such heroes that he believed another might come? Could he really have hoped the Saxons might help him defend the island?

Now I bear the attacks that come, fierce specters of others' desperation. Ambrosius fought well, king of our western states, his army *strang*, no wild band but troops of cohorts with auxiliary cavalry officered by tribunes and prefects...this, the command that came before my own...

The year of my birth, the Saxon broke out of Kent, where they had for so long been contained. The unity of the states had fallen during those years of peace. They struggled to recover. Thinking themselves to be soon overwhelmed, they cried out for a new leader to rally the tribes – the enemy, were fierce warriors, fiercely loyal, who thought a man disgraced to return home once his leader had fallen, who thought it shameful to earn by sweat what could be won by arms.

Our tribesmen of times past fought for home and family, bread and freedom – death or slavery awaiting them in defeat. Knowing their kings would be slain, their villas and cities sacked, their churches and councils swept away, their pasture and wood put to the torch, they fought to restore the only order they had ever known, to rebuild the only promising *woruld* they could remember.

They fought bearing Roman standards. Ambroisus led them. Many died in battle. Many starved. Many took refuge in forest and hills. Many left for the continent. Yet Ambrosius held them together.

Allied with the still powerful church, for seventeen years he provided haven and refuge for the defeated Britons of the eastern province. Secured in his western territories, he imposed a unity of command and purpose by fighting wars of maneuver, and gave strength and hope to the tribesmen.

Now I take up the war, but I am no Roman, and must fight by a different standard. I love too much that greater order the new faith proclaims. And although now a greater peril surrounds us than we have ever known, endangering not only our lives but our truth, it is not yet my time to lean on older arms.

North of the wall, the tribes and clans are bitter, untamed...those three hundred years their mountainous country has preserved their independence.

The Romans watched them, unable to subdue them. And the Picts watched *them*, witnessing the wealth of the Roman traders who came to their land, waiting for the silencing of the Roman trumpets.

On the wall to west, they, too, are hungry...the misty isles of Hibernia across the Irish sea, those wild warriors raiding in their curraughs...

Our eastern border, a Roman border, once defended on the Rhine, now long fallen, and beyond, the thirsting tribes of he crowded continent...they will not ravage this nation.

In the south, on the Saxon shore, they grow stronger yearly.

Once it was *our* forts that stood *strang* along that invasion coast, allowing no landing to go unopposed, no piracy unavenged. Now the seas can no longer protect us. And Rome can do nothing.

Her great civilization, her armies, lie scattered and fallen, though she still seeks like a thief to impose her will through the church. She may succeed. The need of men to think alike is great. As for me, I have my own reasons to fight the godless ones.

Yet her government did serve us well. The tribal areas once independent and hostile now send their royalty each year to the provincial court, even though the Roman states have dissolved and the old monarchies have returned. The population that grew with the occupation remains, Romanized city and villa dwellers, foreigners, settled from all parts of the empire. Barbarians, too, have settled, admitted as allies by Rome and by our own kings, trained in tactics, strategy, and organized warfare – they came as mercenaries, but their loyalty remained to their own chieftains and leaders.

And now they rise up among us as foreigners...

What remains? What is to defend? Who will defend it? The Roman states cannot be rebuilt. The other British kingdoms support my campaigns only until threat to their own lands diminish.

We still have roads. My troops have mobility. The walled towns once empty are now re-garrisoned. The Roman military office I have claimed has withstood the empire's fall.

Our cavalry has been built – Rome used that swift moving shield to counter the blows she was receiving along her vast perimeter, but now I have

14

claimed her knowledge hoard, and made this weapon mine.

But the western kings no longer help me, even fear me, seeking their own power before the nation's, finding no authority in their lives. The power of Roman law has fallen, the church no longer as *strang* as the spirit of man. They return to tribal law, seeking the ancient power, but they do not know the nation.

Where once jeweler and potter labored, forge and foundry now hammer the new destiny, men living to hear the ringing of sweords and the silent screams of rendered flesh.

There must be another way...where is the great teacher? All of you who followed him? The emperors of Rome fed you to the lions, lit their gardens with the burning bodies of your martyrs, and still you would not forswear your faith...now to this land has come those written words, in first form, uncorrupted, of that one you call the Christ.

Somewhere, wherever they may be found, lost or not, I will find them. Those teachings will serve us, or we will serve them...

Cyr Myrddin and his two companions are still quiet, listening to this silence, this silence that wants something of us. Cyr Myrddin, called Emrys, called Merlin, who by many now is considered a god...

Where has the wind gone? That day I met him, I was still a child, and he, unlike any man. Somehow I knew I had never been without him, my first seven years, entrusted to the guardians of his choosing...even then he was teaching me, at times an inner voice speaking aloud, at other times no more than a direction in the wind.

...I was playing in the fields near a stone cottage, amidst the burned stumps of last spring's felled trees. I was frightened when he approached on a black stallion, but lost my fear when he drew close enough for me to see his face. He laid a slender hand on my head, he, who had carried me but hours from my mother's womb – I somehow knew who he was.

He led me into the forest, to a ravine cut into the rock by a rushing stream. He gathered wood to split with his sweord, shaving curled strips and cutting long splinters. With flint and iron, he struck a red ember into a bit of charred cloth, which he laid into the wood, and blew into a blazing *fyr*. He disappeared down into the ravine to throw up large stones from the stream bed, carrying them into the *fyr*. He bent over four saplings, covering them with his cloak, brush, and branches to make a low hut. We waited beside the *fyr* in silence until the stones were glowing red and he carried them into the hut on pieces of bark.

Then we were entering naked, stooping low through the flap door, sitting cross-legged on the damp ground, dark but for the glow of the stones in the shallow pit...he poured water on the rocks and they hissed and filled the air with steam, covering our faces with sweat as our skin burned and we breathed deeper and began a slow chant that seemed never to end, until we plunged outside into a bright icy pool with the current swirling around us, and I wanted to cry out in love and in fear.

When we returned to his horse, my guardians were already awaiting me there with a white colt. For that moment, I held them in my sight, and then rode off with him who would speak to me of my destiny.

Merlin loves the *fyr* and has no fear...death awaits so many, this eve of our battle...this eve of our battle...in youth and ignorance I once fathered a son, against the laws of man and nature. Why has no other come to wipe that memory from me? It has been more than a decade. Still, I fear some frightful visitation must descend from it.

Now I hear my men, speaking of the last few hundred yards needed to top the ridge – the way grows too steep for the road builders! For more than a mile they have built the oaken ramps.

...the hollow thudding of wood upon wood now ceases – those ramps for our chargers, a thousand wooden planks hauled up the mountainside to lie upon a frame of post and beam, a narrow path clinging to the final rise of earthen cliffs.

He never speaks at times like these. I respect his silence. His words come so rarely these months. What danger lies ahead? He offers no guidance, not now. Only he has told me, I alone hold the reins of Britain's destiny, while his *weorc* is near completion. Be without fear, he has said, but I fear, knowing his wisdom is of the heavens, and I have yet learned little of his power.

A few things he has taught me well; these will always be close to me. A few things are yet to come; for these I will listen.

As for the rest, I rely now upon my own vision, though it be only the vision of one man, it is by the claims of the blood of a hundred tribes that my heart beats.

Cyr Myrddin and his two companions...some ancient instinct joins them, a silent language greater than words, dwelling in a night more real than day, roaming even now, hunting on the moors under stars as moonshadows grow longer. They know him alone and trust no other man. While others fear them, they fear no man, and hold great knowledge, the taste of every stream in the forest, living by different laws and means, yet with greater justice. They are never far from him.

His understandings could never be mine. He has struggled and paid greatly for his knowledge, surpassing even the wordhoard of the Druids. That *woruld* he beholds so strange other men tremble before it, have died in seeking it –

There! To the ridgecrest! The ramps are completed, my troops emerging. The Saxons will be prepared for neither the time nor place of my coming!

I fight by my own wisdom now, born of the ancient power of the tribes, and by a new power, born of the sacred covenant.

The earth beneath us thunders. The night speaks in the whipping wind, across the mountainside in cavernous echoes and explosions...their drums rising, too, from the valley floor, the beating, pounding, no sound, no cry, but the Saxon drums fill my ears until my blood pounds, too. Soon all will learn whose drums beat louder – ringing sweords our answer to heathen!

Many this night will find passage, Saxons and Britons alike – worthy death we will give them, though it be as well the day of our discovery.

What will remain? All we thought we might become...going forth to destroy our past and redeem it, finding our courage in the flames of tomorrow's dawn that we pass through leaving all things burned and forgotten, seeking our chosen birth and the blood that bore us, for tomorrow the *fyr*, tomorrow the first day.

Where are my generals?

My shoulder-companions?

Who can speak now, against this laden loud silence?

Yes, four-legged consort of Cyr Myrddin, your word true and wild, longthroat howling shattering the ridge top to fall upon the plain below.

warlight born

Darkness peers through dim silverglint of blademetal – my sweord lying at hand, forged of skyfallen stone by the smiths of an earlier race. Faithful since found, long has it served setting edge to edge against heathen blade. Not yet has it failed me.

Fyr low. Flames gone elsewhere, the gray mountainrock still, breathing colder air birthed of other cry than the valley below. Ridge falling on the westward running...on the eastward climbs, gathers thrusts of stones emerging in distant towers. Down, my *weorc*.

Footsteps war-gear laden advance, falling across the frozen rock. He speaks standing, features forming in the light of the slow moving flames. "The ramps are ready, Arturus."

As he departs with my nod, I breathe out my held concern – night's unthinkable task done, my cavalry conquering earth's risen ridgewall – his words still loud in my ears as I rise from the *fyr* and hours of grounddamp into the chill night air, nearer the dim stars of the ashen sky.

I still remember, have not forgotten. Seeking my way back along the ridge to that rainpool in the rock hollow, my eyes grope the darkness, steps searching until at last the shapes appear, that smooth place of white ice crust among the rock shadows.

To lay down my robes before thin ice cracks with my naked plunge, my blood cold pierced, sinking above my waist. With the cask I have brought to restore my upper body, I pour the water over my chest and head, my flesh protesting until breath and heart

23

heave to rekindle bloodheat, and the *fyr* fills me. Draughts of night air like wind course through my limbs as I climb from the pool to stand under stars upon rock.

Warm, my cloak, as I throw it over me to walk back to a *fyr* now embers, my companions gone.

Stillness joins me.

Kneeling beside the coals to gird my loins, taking ashes to darken my eye sockets, I sit within my cloak before my altar – my shield leaning upon a stone, emblem dim in the starlight, a face and halo...called Holy Mother, who bore the child not of man, carry us forth in battle for their defeat, grant the holy *fyr* fill our arms, bear us on in the madness we summon to abide your *weorc*.

My war-gear laid between wool cloths before eveningfall, ground-strengthened now, I ready war tools and battledress.

Many of us have already found that greater life beyond this one, but I have much to do before that rest be granted me...slipping on the linen undergarment, pulling on wool tunic, shortbreeches, a leather apron for my waist, and my smithcraft summons, shining of ring braid, forge-knit battle shirt of mail, hard-linked and hammered. So many blows it has kept from my chest, a worthy bloodkeeper that serves better than the rest. Leather thongs thrice wrapped around legs securing sandals to feet, and a deerskin tunic, stone embroidered and gilt-edged, won by deeds – I had joy of Ambrosius, a worthy ring-giver. Upon my head a smooth Roman helmet, polished to glimmering.

I reach for black bearskin mantle hung upon ground-sunk spear – that beast I fought to steal his anger, so his jaws might rest upon my forehead and his fore claws across my chest. With gloves of leather and mail upon my hands, and my sheathed sweord secured to body harness, I hear the footsteps come again.

"We are ready to descend, my lord."

He knows my answer as I walk away, toward a rise on the ridge, the rocks slipping, and the earth crumbling underfoot. I have always needed, will always need, to so ready myself. To walk toward the black silver-chested clouds moving upon the blue darkness, to find the standing place, to look down upon the vale of a thousand *fyrs*, feeling upon my face the wind's slight passage steady over the ridgecrest...as I begin to sway, forward and back, side to side, then in small circles, in smaller and smaller circles, rooting my feet into the rock, at last to stand without effort, without memory, without thought...

I draw my sweord and raise it heavenward, right hand above left on the hilt, wrists to forehead, holding time, wind passing, nightclouds restless...my men below emerging along ridge's far edge, mounted warriors burdening the high tablelands, as my arms move upward to full height with my gaze holding the valley below, and wait to breathe the slow fall of locked arms as sweordtip touches ground.

And I draw it up again to throw a long slow swing, shoulder leading forearm around my waist, bearing it on, completing the circle overhead to slash down across the body right to left, slowly, drawing it to the left shoulder slashing down to right knee, draw to right shoulder, slash to left knee, left shoulder, right knee, upper body winding back into stillness and uncoiling to pivot a half turn upon a right step, carrying the swing of sweord full around on straight locked arms, and another step, following the sweord's weight to seal the ring, and the blade passes to the left to bring the force in a high backlash right, and hold, the breath, and the wind over arms, over valley, lowering my sweord to listen with closed eyes, breathing full...

Fyr be near. Open, eyes, upon my conquest. Join me, wind.

Turning back to my ready war-band, I descend to meet the forming ranks of my chieftains, horses and men in full battle-array of iron and leather. Their silent salute of sweord and spear held high overhead I acknowledge with a glance. Our battle plans laid long ago, I, too, hold silence strongest.

I walk to the *fyr* to take my ground-driven spear – to find a black raven perched upon its base.

"The arms carrier! Bring the arms carrier!" My command passing through the ranks.

"My lord?"

"Four spears!"

While my chieftains watch, he goes and returns, standing them before me. I pick up the first, holding it overhead with wide grip, and snap it in two. And the same with the second, and the third, until the forth resists me, holds *strang*.

"Burn the others."

My black stallion awaiting me, twenty hands to hold my height. I grip his cold reins and mount, high upon *strang* charger greater than any. Snorting mist, he knows the task, shares the war lust...with certain pace carrying me to the outer edge of the tableland, where the earth becomes a slope falling off into the darkness below, and beyond into the *fyr*-lit plain of their camp below. My troops follow, nine abreast, one hundred deep, hooves knocking on the frozen groundrock. The Saxon force is only four times our number.

I signal the column to a halt with a raised arm, and wait as the command runs back down the line, rank to rank the horses holding, noises of hooves at last receding to the rear. Cohorts all quiet again. Listening through the night, I am unsure, battlesense uneasy...nothing...but I am mistrustful of this silence...

My hands fall back to the reins as my lead pulls the troops into a single column. My steed finding his own way over the ridge to begin the descent of the steep shale slope, and the others follow. The first forty yards...stones above clattering, horses slipping, fearful, while firm hands try to forestall the fright. Behind, loud whinnying from those mounts approaching the steep pitch, and still louder, against the will of their riders.

"The chargers will not dare the pitch!"
"We cannot go down!"
"We must abandon the attack!"
"Our night's labor wasted!"

"HOLD!" My eyes search the slope. There is no other path, no answer for my men, eager war-band restless for battle. We must fight. We must descend. Again, my eyes sweeping the slope, for anything, unable to think – Myrddin?

A cloaked hooded figure on the ridge, in dim outline against the sky, walking across the front line. A chieftain reins his steed around to hear his words, then pulls him up into the saddle and disappears beyond the land's edge. Above, the clouds shift slowly upon the dark sky. There could yet be some hope. I wait, watching the *fyrs* like red glowing stars far below, to learn if our chosen course might be granted us. Growing cold, looking again to the ridgecrest, none of the war band above now visible.

At last! They return, waving my men on! To continue the descent! Cyr Myrddin's plan become's visible, the smaller island-bred horses strung between the excited chargers. They begin again. A charger looses its footing, falls, throwing the rider. Unhurt, he tries to calm the beast, helping it to stand. Feint gray clouds rising now from the valley, the horses go on, the minutes longer for those above me on uneasy mounts, stones sliding down the slope, the column winding its way down the narrow, barely visible shelves made by the lead of my mount upon the deep piled stones, until the first hour passes...

And a slight lessening of slope with wary horses picking a trail through sharp scattered shrubs, the riders still watchful, the way slow...until far below the long awaited sight arises, the forest's edge, dim lit by the half-moon.

Stones trickling, the column behind a serpent rising, vanishing into a dark line on the heights. Stars shining like crystal stones sharp set in black. Another hour has passed, the wood reached, the pitch now less, horses finding firm-footing on the ground leafcrust crisp-frosted under hoof...branches dragging, snapping, damp sweet of rotting leaves and the musk of horse sweat, threading down some unseen path, glint of starlight on the bare icy branches...fog of breath before my eyes...

Three hundred of the counselors of Vortigernus died at the banquet table, by the hands of the Saxons who sat beside them, who came to seal the pact of peace with sudden murder...

Hooting owls disturbed fly up...no end to their slaughter, taking the forts at Anderita, Dubris, Regulrium, killing counts and noblemen – even kings have fallen before their red tide.

Trees some cover, only the stronger stars still out, heavens dull-hammered silver in the earliest dawn. Slope softening, trees scattering into the low foothills at mountain base...small groves and open patches of earth, covered with bunchgrass, laid down by the frost.

Now the hill gentle, tall yellow brown grass brushing the bellies of our horses, crossing stony creeks into a still thinner wood, dark posts of trees against the lightening sky. Webs of branchcrossings form in dawn light, while through trees on the far horizon bright silver rises from a border of white.

29

There! The square huts of their camp across the valley floor!

I lead my men advancing to the last stream at slope's bottom, ice-patched, slow moving, waiting as the column descends through the wood to reform on stream's edge, ranks again close and deep. Murmuring of chieftains now recalling the battle plan, scuffling of hooves, snorting breaths...

As another forest grows within the wood, as we raise them high, hundreds of shafts of spears, mailcoats clinking, horses shifting uneasily, streamwater pouring...

"Cei, their chieftain's name," my only request.

"Dagra," his reply.

Unsheathing my sweord to raise it heavenward, my shout follows, "To worthy death!"

"To worthy death!" my thirty chieftains cry.

Then the silence long, as I look to them one by one, meeting their eyes...a few birds calling...across the stream, a wind rising...

UNBRIDLED!

LUNGING MY HORSE FORWARD BOUNDING IN FURY – STREAM ICE CRACKING FLIES UP UNDER HOOVES TRAMPLING. EXPLODES THE DAWN QUIET IN WAR CRIES – BIRDS ERUPT FROM TREES IN HUGE CLOUDS. RAGE ESCAPING THE WOOD RUNNING ONTO PLAIN, HORSES WILD GALLOPING – MY WAR BAND LEADS THE CHARGE, WIND RISING AS WE RIDE, RISING BECOMES TORRENT, FALLS OVER US, FILLS OUR EARS RUSHING IN MINDS,

30

AND REINING HARDER, BEATING THE GROUNDDRUM, DRIVEN INTO SADDLES THIGHS TIGHT TO FLANKS, OUR BURNING BLAZED INTO THE MUSCLES OF HORSES, WHILE ROARS IN OUR THROAT OUR ETERNITY SEEKING, WITH WAR-CRIES MATCHING THE WIND'S STEADY FURY AS WE RIDE, OUTFLOWING, FRONT LINE BROADER AND BROADER AS THE RANKS EMERGE, SURGING SWIFT THICK-MANED STALLIONS SWEEPING ATHWART, HOOF-THUNDER THE BATTLE CRY OF HORSES, WAR HORNS THE SOUNDING OF OUR HEAVEN'S WRATH, WE, THE WIND BENEATH BLACK CLOUD SKY!

Betrayed! Betrayed! No spy's *weorc* this – foot-soldiers made ready in throngs upon the plain – but certain word of our attack bartered for tongue-gold!

"BORS! TO THE FLANKS!" My cry rings out above the din. "Our center will not hold!"

Our advantage lost, only with courage can we now meet their far greater number. Our front line of charge gallops steady, covering the movement behind. Our force shifting outward, clods of earth fly, mounts turning to mass upon our torrent's edge, the land dipping before the horizon of the Saxon dark battlefront, and we ride on toward the shadow of four thousand.

One shadow becomes four – the tribes. Four becomes eighty – the clans. Eighty becomes the tribesmen – two hundred score – many soon to find uneasy passage in chill and bitter fame, once joined on the bloodpath brandishing dark iron. Battle horns louder urge the striking-at-foe! Blood for our destiny! Blood for our tribes! Food for our soil, the thirsty turned sod! Bloodpools dark seeping will be the coming Saxon glory!

Fools to meet my charge, my war band loves fierce reaping! Almighty lord lead us conquering!

Our advancing storm upon the heathen shieldwall, our spears slung by arm force upon swift charge of steed splitting their shieldboards. Their first line falls by iron-tipped flight – those shadows of men, no faces to be seen in the dim mornlight, and the floodtides meet crashing in thunder, sweords smashing to hardwood...horses wild, high arcs of battle-axes swing upon riders. Hundreds fall in bitter clashing, under hooves cracking bone.

First man I reach my sweord red flame at throat, no utterance, he dies, and on, and on, the press of battle – to the next, slashing chest, he falls, clash iron to iron, my blade the stronger rips bone and sinew, makes the slain three, loud the ring of sweord to shield. The second blow shatters, breaks through to face while another attacks – I crash down to sing the iron, note upon note the metal's strain, with my swifter singing blade striking down a good warrior.

All around, shadow upon shadow, *woruld candel* yet below earth...sideways I swing metal edge to lay open a skull. On the ground, around the dead, red pools now mingle, good blood of two nations, and on!

My companions hew men like rushes, none standing the strokes of their wolf-fury, hearts bent to fighting, soaking the fields, making carrion for crows – a spear thrust to my back struck aside by Cei's watchful sweord. With my steed hurtling ahead, my blade cleaves a jaw, rises high, crashes down through shield to shoulder. Against the spear driving toward me, I wheel my mount to cut the Saxon shaft through, and striking down, my blow breaks the iron helmet.

Our chargers rush onward, trampling the fallen, their first line broken. A sweord thrusting at Cei misses the mark – leaning down I swing my sweord to sever the backbone. Our steeds lunge through the second line shattering shield-wall, boards broken to bits beneath hard hooves, while still their war-hard warriors stand the harsh trial, not fearing iron and edge. Lashed to frenzy, they bear forth their fierce battle-axes.

My shoulder-companions not trembling before Saxon blades shout commands above the battle-din, bending thought to handwork, to meet the Saxons where they throng thickest, our tribesmen ruthless in strife as they swarm upon us.

We fight, our strokes fiercer, roundshields clenched in finger-grip, our blows scattering weapons, striking at bodies blood-spurting and the finer spray from flailing sweords, but their axes now begin their death-biting. Two of my band fall, and their assault grows bolder, our horses caught in the hordes, their axes rushing to splinter shields. More of mine are cut down by dripping battle-axes. Our battle-weariness grows while the coming barbarians remain *strang*, not weakened by battle's first war-play – their companions have borne the brunt with blood so by greater number they might yet prevail. Over the greater expanse, the war-bands of my chieftains hold the field against heathen horde, but many are falling, war gear strewn trampled on stiff mud, bright tunics bloodied and dirt-covered, while the *woruld candel* rises on the glittering mailcoats of fallen dead, who now have found their fair claim to that greater fortune.

My companions moving as one gather closer round me to resist the rising onslaught. A spear grazes my helmet. Next to me, dragged from his horse, a hearth companion falls, head loosed by battle-axe, my rage rearing my steed ahead to rain blows upon shoulders – with three strokes I kill three, and with a thrust of sweordtip under bonecage lift a heathen chieftain from mount to let him fall dead from my blade and cry out my anger-song. My horse ham-stringed collapses as I leap landing upright, my sweord crashing through skull to jaw, and turning swing with two arms to cleave a linden shield in two, and him with it. At my right shoulder, an attacker – my sweord backlashing crashes flat against his chest, knocking him down. Cei leaps from his mount with dagger to slash his throat, as all around my war band dismounts as the swarming of the heathen horde locks rigid our horses' free rein.

Dagra, said to possess the strength of twenty. Dagra. Where flies the banner of his war band? A battle-axe swinging against my chest, my blade meets the shaft withholding the stroke while my grip finds his throat, crushing breath to toss him aside. There! The banner distant! Guarded by his fierce clan of legend! 1 want them all! Sweord of a mounted chieftain falling upon me, I throw it back high with an upward stroke, slash across ripping open the breastplate and the flesh beneath. A battleaxe plunging toward my face Cei turns aside, forcing it outward glancing off the mailcoat upon my shoulder, and I run my sweord through his chest.

Aldric falls, great battle friend. A Saxon fallen to his knees thrusts upward for me. My kick to the helmeted head snaps his neck. Another attacking meets my two-armed backlash and falls, as I turn into sweord meeting sweord overhead, blade against blade my blow the stronger carries down through neck and shoulders. Collapsing he leaves me unguarded to face a Saxon-aimed spear – Bevydyr hurls first, his sweord rupturing the belly. I throw him my shortsweord, and turn as a spear thrust rips through my mailcoat, cuts high, tearing through mail to graze my bonecage. My blood begins to run – Dagra! Stepping aside from the sweord thrust to my chest, I grasp his hilt and pull his body through my blade.

Horses riderless caught in battle-flay rearing, raising fearful cries, and the sweetish smell of blood filling the warming air in the mists of sweat and breath – Cei and Bevydyr step before me, a moment's shield, time enough to draw one breath, and another.

"Dagra!" my war cry rising above the battle noise as I stride forth, slash down and swing across, two dead – an axe blow – I cannot – my shoulder sliced open in spray of blood.

Cedric hearing my gasp steps before me before the barbarian can finish his *weorc*, flies his sweordtip across his throat. Bevydyr steps back again to cover my side. Dalde falls, belly pierced by ripping lance. I lay my edge into his killer's heathen jaw, sending bonechips and smashed teeth flying while another sweord swings for my face – throwing back my face I feel only its wind passing and step forward to thrust two-armed into his chest, hot blood wetting my hand as I heave my blade out of his body to let that Saxon corpse crash at my feet, and stepping over it throw my sweord broadside against highfalling axe to knock shaft from grip, my downstroke returning bites into his neck red-showering. Maldred falls, head cleaved by axe stroke. Cei sends the slayer on.

Lifting my gaze over the battleplain, the fallen dead lie behind *their* lines – they are driving us back. Let roar my savage cry to loose heathen head, cleave another down to his neck. Cei strikes down another, Bevydyr two. On the ground, the heaps of bloody flesh pile into mounds.

More of them! Hundreds hiding in the hillside, rushing down upon us a fearsome torrent shaking shield and axe, hailing harsh war cries. Young Feowulf, throat torn by lance brings his hand to hold his lifeblood, falls! 1 will avenge that kinsmen! Behind me, two are upon Cei. I turn swinging full to lay open the back, Bevydyr protecting my rear.

The new horde of barbarians massing on the eastern flank, our tribesmen begin to fall, giving ground, their will weakening –

"CEI!" I give him the command, "DAGRA!"

Cei hands on the charge, shouting to my war-band that follows me in full run driving deep into the Saxon ranks with our wedge of raised shields. My forty breaking through their lines leave the battlefront far behind as they close in around us, and I hurl words into the battle din.

"NO FEAR FOR US! THOUGH THIS DAY WE MEET FIERCE PASSAGE, IT IS TO OUR GREATER GLORY!"

Onward to the shieldwall built by their watchful clan leaders seeing our charge! The surrounding Saxon press their advantage, seeking our banner! My eyes meet Cei's – he shouts, "IS OUR STRUGGLE ENDED HERE, LAID LOW BY HEATHEN IRON?"

The outer ring of my war band breaking, six companions of many a campaign fallen slain, now three more, and two, and four. The inner ring wavers, begins to shatter. Cei and Bevydyr still *strang* swing sweords hawkswift in the air, shadows flashing darkly loose the war-harness of Weird-singled men. Our inner ring breached, we form our last shieldwall against their fury, but Dedra falls, Maldric, Adowld, Esson – dead by our betrayer – I will live to seek him out. Nau, Daeth, Kendall, my finest warriors fall from their heathen onslaught yet bolder, our only deliverance now the dark passage of the Otherworld.

"Heathen! For you a fearful victory!" Cei's sweord is knocked from his grip. With bare hand to cut short the blow of falling axe, he wrenches free the shaft, crashing a mailed fist into the attacker's face to sends him stumbling. Bevydyr slashing fells another.

"BEVYDYR!"

My warning too late, the unholy axe swings against his bone cage bursting through mail. Longest my hearth companion, he reaches one hand to his bloodied chest – Cei strikes down the murderer – and falls, the man more than any other I have loved – no, let vengeance be sweeter than sorrow!

Spear-lunge thrust aside by my roundshield, stepping aside from another, taking hold of the shaft pull him onto my sweord, I grab the spear from his hand to drive it hard into the belly of another. These gasps and cries the music I ring from heathen souls – they will come to fear my song!

"CEI! Above!"

Turning, he blocks the blow with shield, cuts short the next, swinging axe to axe scraping iron, drives round again to sink his blade into the shoulder, leaving it embedded stoops for his sweord.

"Fair warning, my lord!" Cei yells in thanks.

Swinging my sweord circling overhead into horned helmet to side-split the skull, to another, feinting the same stroke, I cut the bonecage instead. All around my men are finding their swift passage to the Otherworld, and the barbarians are still massing.

A chieftain advances boldly and we meet broadsweords ringing, iron upon iron, my blade the swifter thudding to bone, but he fights fiercer, clashes above, bellows. Bounding back from the stroke, I reverse my next blow crossing my arms overhead to backlash swinging swifter than his sweord can follow. My blade flies through his hip, and I meet the next sweord advancing, slashing a half-circle to smash the blade from his hand, swinging back at bared breast to cut deep through the breastplate opening the bloodseam, while I suck breath from the air burning cold, my fists blood-covered, frozen to the hilt, my strokes yet *strang*.

Senda falls, six years my shoulder-companion.

"Dagra!"

My blow shears an arm, he falls after it – for you a red embrace! My shield bears an axe blow, and another, and the next falling short leans him into me, his chest bared to my two-armed thrust I sink my blade deep. Still embedded, it bears without breaking the bite of another axe – pushing the flesh from my iron with foot, its edge meets the next blow falling splintering the shaft and driving on to the jaw.

"LORD!"

Maldred, my youngest warrior call, standing weaponless before a Saxon giant. I cannot reach him. The barbarian grasping his breastplate and helmet to bare his throat, bites tearing to breath and blood passage, lifting the body by the harness and casting it down to laugh a mouth of red dripping. I know that shileldcrest, Athel the Wolf. The time of our meeting will come. Against axe swinging low, my balance cannot recover – AAAAAHHH! Bonechips and flesh sliced from my knee, blood pouring,

"NOOOOOO!"

Great breaths arise and *fyr* comes filling, danceof-light-madness erupts to God-strength, blinding, until other eyes open – to see the striking place, storm the unguarded pathway, blood singing the faith! Misfortune to the first who blocks my way – my stroke cross gliding severs body from legs, and the flame still brighter, letting my sweord fall, my hands to do the *weorc*. Taking hold of the heathen arm driving axe against me, I twist bone to shoulder and grab for his war-harness to thrust his body high into the air, hurling him against the heathen shields, and reach to the ground for the fallen axe.

Two fall as I advance, and I strike another to tear the shoulder through. With long stride reaching to grip his throat I crush the flesh into a rattling grasp of failing breath. An axe shearing against my back tears open my mailshirt, scraping skin from bone – another knocks my sword from my grasp. Swinging around to drive the iron-banded heel of my hand against his face to snap the neck, my elbow slams back into another throat.

"Arturus!"

Cei's swift hand throws my sweord back into my grip to race the descending axe as my sweord flashes one-handed to his temple

"Dagra!"

My knee weakening, this blood for the tribes...why do you stumble? Holy Virgin, I pray, I pray let the bloodflow end, and roar –

"Dagra!"

Why these short breaths, so strained? With me not yet worthy to perish. My eyes' clear sight

40

returning, I see my shoulder-companions surrounding me. Little glory for them, only honor for their children, as they bear the blows falling on all sides, as I fall one knee to the ground, warm blood into cold mud, leaning on my sweord forcing longer breaths, over and over, knowing the next fury my last, no blood for muscle and limbs.

Sky lightening into day, dawn colors fading, as I push myself up by my sweord, to rush forth into the flay – against the first Saxon, my mail-gloved fist crashing into his face, knocking him from his feet to send him sprawling, back swiping with open palm to knock loose another lunging sweord and lift him one-handed to throw him aside.

"Dagra!"

Our last rushing, Aldric falls, Brent beside him, but now – it is his war band! Dagra's!

My cry rises above the metal clashing, "DAGRA!"

All hear my roar of bloodlust as I rush to challenge their lord, robed in hides and gold. With eyes of ice he stands, a head taller than me, me who has stood always a head taller than any.

"You are mine, Dagra," I make the first boast.

"You are far from home, young one," he answers.

Striding forth, he attacks clashing sweords, swift blades of no fear and strike! Again! Again! Overhead, he meets my downstroke with downstroke shearing edge to edge driving down against me. Blow by blow we advance the war-play, until I force his blade out beyond my shoulder to follow my stroke upon his – I unstring the striking arm that falls blood-spurting onto the ground.

His words, "Fair blow, Briton, that arm had itself severed many."

In the rising of my savage cry I drive my hilt through his belly with my forward stride, and stride again bearing him, and stride again flinging him from my sweord hearing my cry ending, falling into the battle sounds, into shapes and dim colors glowing in my eyes.

Sweet, the unheard sounds, this place, this time.

War, I am, war that makes me.

Cei slays the banner holder, their flag falling sending tremors through the heathen ranks. My war-clan, *strang* again with Dagra's blood, fights on fearless, claiming the lives of his shoulder-companions.

The last warriors of his worthy band join together fiercer now in war-whetted anger to avenge their lord – only death will keep them from their task, as twice our number surrounds us, so far from our tribesmen.

My tribesmen of new hope, seeing the center struck, begin to hold their ground as the heathen weaken at the war-play.

But our arms failing, unable to find one moment of recovery, and my hearth-companions begin to fall, all of us trapped without our mounts.

Yet they will long remember this morning *weorc* of ours – Cei's sweord arm slashed to the bone, he falters – stepping between them I pierce the bonecage, thrusting upward, and push the body from my sweord, as I prepare for the next assault.

"Where is Gawain?" Cei cries out, his words weak.

Bretold struck down, Cardor, Senlaw, Rolde, more.

"GAWAIN!" My voice forced above the battle-din, standing beside Cei, still swinging his sweord with one arm, as more Saxons surround us, shaking high-held axes, and with a war cry sound our charge –

"SHORTSWEORDS!"

Hilts raised high, our broadsweords fly as spears, find their mark in Saxon flesh, and we draw shortsweords rushing to fight in yet closer quarters, cramping their swings – before they can draw daggers, we run them through.

Gawain, where are you? I strain to hear the approaching war horns of his troops on the near plain – nothing, only the dawn gusts.

We are far behind the enemy line, heathen helmets surrounding us for hundreds of yards. Broadsweords gone, the near Saxon slain, we are sure to fall before the next onslaught of axe and spear – another war band raises their harsh cry against us and charges!

GROUND THUNDERING MOUNTS CUT SHORT THE ATTACK! Gawain's column emerging from the Saxon swarm meets the charge, lays down the foot soldiers, as our tribesmen following pour through the way made open by him, cutting their army in half.

The less courageous Saxon begin to flee, to be

hewn down by our riders on the flanks. Our fresh troops far stronger of body and spirit bear their shields forward wielding sure sweords, forge amongst them scattering blows, laying the last hundreds down.

Horses given us, we ride for their settlement, my band rushing war-hungry in victory. Reaching their wattle huts, we set them afire with the flames burning in their own hearths, my men gathering the furs and weapons that remain, searching for the stores of grain.

A tall boy frightened by Cei's approach runs out from behind a haystack to escape – stepping into his path he runs into me full square, as I clamp my hand down upon his shoulder, his long blond hair in waves, blue eyes, tall, soon to be a man.

I let the fear pass from him until he is calm, until he lifts his eyes to meet my gaze, his breaths now slow and deep.

I do him this honor.

Naked webbed branches outlined in the low light of the *woruld candel*, my breath hard, blowing gray vapor.

He nods, proudly accepting his fate, and I run him through the chest. He collapses at my feet as I meet the eyes of Perceval and Cei who stand watching. The morning wind gusts between us, and is understanding enough.

I return with them to the field of my conquering, corpse strewn, crops set afire. We walk over the stubble of autumn-reaped corn, where my men now gather the bodies into piles for burning. Our tribesmen we leave in full harness and armor with their weapons, the Saxons we strip of their war-gear, and for Dagra...

"Build a pyre, full dress, sweord, helmet, and breastplate – give his ashes to the wind."

...walking on through bloodied fields, with sky above dark silver broad rippling and the light of day dim, *candel* hidden by cloud now.

Behind us, the columns of black smoke meet the near darkness above, Anwnn of the Wild Hunt soon to bear them on to the next *woruld* of their inhabiting.

Iron-sown field, now silent but for the calling of the ravens, carrion eager.

These were my men, these are my men, these men I love. I live, and they die. They fight, and I am called warrior. It will be long before they hear again the strains of harp at meadhall. Forever, I carry these men with me forever.

My vision, my word, has brought them to this, their last battlefield, this plain of passage. Now in the flowing from their wounds is the blood of my vision born. From their silenced war-cries, my kingdom draws breath.

Who am I to so ask of them? Do I alone bear claim to the greater *weorc*?

Has it been given me?

I am Arthur.

It has been given me.

END